The Boxcar Children Mysteries

THE BOXCAR CHILDREN
SURPRISE ISLAND
THE YELLOW HOUSE MYSTERY
MYSTERY RANCH
MIKE'S MYSTERY
BLUE BAY MYSTERY
THE WOODSHED MYSTERY
THE LIGHTHOUSE MYSTERY
MOUNTAIN TOP MYSTERY
SCHOOLHOUSE MYSTERY
CABOOSE MYSTERY
HOUSEBOAT MYSTERY
SNOWBOUND MYSTERY
TREE HOUSE MYSTERY
BICYCLE MYSTERY
MYSTERY IN THE SAND
MYSTERY BEHIND THE WALL
BUS STATION MYSTERY
BENNY UNCOVERS A MYSTERY
THE HAUNTED CABIN MYSTERY
THE DESERTED LIBRARY MYSTERY
THE ANIMAL SHELTER MYSTERY
THE OLD MOTEL MYSTERY
THE MYSTERY OF THE HIDDEN
   PAINTING
THE AMUSEMENT PARK MYSTERY
THE MYSTERY OF THE MIXED-UP ZOO
THE CAMP-OUT MYSTERY
THE MYSTERY GIRL
THE MYSTERY CRUISE
THE DISAPPEARING FRIEND MYSTERY
THE MYSTERY OF THE SINGING GHOST
MYSTERY IN THE SNOW
THE PIZZA MYSTERY
THE MYSTERY HORSE
THE MYSTERY AT THE DOG SHOW
THE CASTLE MYSTERY
THE MYSTERY OF THE LOST VILLAGE
THE MYSTERY ON THE ICE
THE MYSTERY OF THE PURPLE POOL
THE GHOST SHIP MYSTERY

THE MYSTERY IN WASHINGTON, DC
THE CANOE TRIP MYSTERY
THE MYSTERY OF THE HIDDEN BEACH
THE MYSTERY OF THE MISSING CAT
THE MYSTERY AT SNOWFLAKE INN
THE MYSTERY ON STAGE
THE DINOSAUR MYSTERY
THE MYSTERY OF THE STOLEN MUSIC
THE MYSTERY AT THE BALL PARK
THE CHOCOLATE SUNDAE MYSTERY
THE MYSTERY OF THE HOT
   AIR BALLOON
THE MYSTERY BOOKSTORE
THE PILGRIM VILLAGE MYSTERY
THE MYSTERY OF THE STOLEN
   BOXCAR
THE MYSTERY IN THE CAVE
THE MYSTERY ON THE TRAIN
THE MYSTERY AT THE FAIR
THE MYSTERY OF THE LOST MINE
THE GUIDE DOG MYSTERY
THE HURRICANE MYSTERY
THE PET SHOP MYSTERY
THE MYSTERY OF THE SECRET MESSAGE
THE FIREHOUSE MYSTERY
THE MYSTERY IN SAN FRANCISCO
THE NIAGARA FALLS MYSTERY
THE MYSTERY AT THE ALAMO
THE OUTER SPACE MYSTERY
THE SOCCER MYSTERY
THE MYSTERY IN THE OLD ATTIC
THE GROWLING BEAR MYSTERY
THE MYSTERY OF THE LAKE MONSTER
THE MYSTERY AT PEACOCK HALL
THE WINDY CITY MYSTERY
THE BLACK PEARL MYSTERY
THE CEREAL BOX MYSTERY
THE PANTHER MYSTERY
THE MYSTERY OF THE QUEEN'S JEWELS
THE STOLEN SWORD MYSTERY
THE BASKETBALL MYSTERY

The Movie Star Mystery
The Mystery of the Pirate's Map
The Ghost Town Mystery
The Mystery of the Black Raven
The Mystery in the Mall
The Mystery in New York
The Gymnastics Mystery
The Poison Frog Mystery
The Mystery of the Empty Safe
The Home Run Mystery
The Great Bicycle Race Mystery
The Mystery of the Wild Ponies
The Mystery in the Computer
   Game
The Mystery at the Crooked
   House
The Hockey Mystery
The Mystery of the Midnight Dog
The Mystery of the Screech Owl
The Summer Camp Mystery
The Copycat Mystery
The Haunted Clock Tower
   Mystery
The Mystery of the Tiger's Eye
The Disappearing Staircase
   Mystery
The Mystery on Blizzard
   Mountain
The Mystery of the Spider's Clue
The Candy Factory Mystery
The Mystery of the Mummy's
   Curse
The Mystery of the Star Ruby
The Stuffed Bear Mystery
The Mystery of Alligator Swamp
The Mystery at Skeleton Point
The Tattletale Mystery
The Comic Book Mystery
The Great Shark Mystery
The Ice Cream Mystery
The Midnight Mystery

The Mystery in the Fortune
   Cookie
The Black Widow Spider Mystery
The Radio Mystery
The Mystery of the Runaway
   Ghost
The Finders Keepers Mystery
The Mystery of the Haunted
   Boxcar
The Clue in the Corn Maze
The Ghost of the Chattering
   Bones
The Sword of the Silver Knight
The Game Store Mystery
The Mystery of the Orphan Train
The Vanishing Passenger
The Giant Yo-Yo Mystery
The Creature in Ogopogo Lake
The Rock 'n' Roll Mystery
The Secret of the Mask
The Seattle Puzzle
The Ghost in the First Row
The Box That Watch Found
A Horse Named Dragon
The Great Detective Race
The Ghost at the Drive-In Movie
The Mystery of The Traveling
   Tomatoes
The Spy Game
The Dog-Gone Mystery
The Vampire Mystery
Superstar Watch
The Spy in the Bleachers
The Amazing Mystery Show

THE MYSTERY OF THE SINGING GHOST

created by
GERTRUDE CHANDLER WARNER

Illustrated by Charles Tang

Albert Whitman & Company
Chicago, Illinois

ISBN 978-0-8075-5398-5

20 19 LB 15 14 13 12 11 10

Printed in the U.S.A.

Contents

CHAPTER   PAGE

1. The Old House   1
2. Work! Work! Work!   12
3. The Singing   25
4. The Argument   35
5. The Mysterious Dress   45
6. The Diary   63
7. Aunt Jane Arrives   73
8. The Letter   84
9. The Back Stairs   96
10. Where is Celia?   106

CHAPTER 1

The Old House

The Alden children and their cousins Joe and Alice Alden stood in front of an old house on the edge of Greenfield. They looked up and down at the three-story, gray-shingled home. It needed painting. The porch steps were broken and the windows on each of the three floors were a different shape.

Six-year-old Benny shook his head. "This sure is a funny-looking house," he said.

Joe laughed. "I guess it is. But this house

was built in 1900 and in those days houses didn't look like they do now."

Joe's wife, Alice, walked up the four steps that led to the wide porch. "The real estate agent gave me the key," she said. "Let's go in."

The children followed Alice inside. They all walked through the dusty living room and dining room. Ten-year-old Violet ran her fingers over an old table that was in the living room. "This place could use a good dusting," she said.

Henry, who was fourteen, said, "Well, I heard the agent tell Joe and Alice that no one has lived in the house for years."

They all walked into a small room with walls covered with empty bookshelves. A huge desk that took up half the room was against one wall. A dead plant was on the floor.

Jessie said seriously, "In all my twelve years I've never seen a place as strange as this one."

Alice moved toward the door. "We haven't

even been upstairs yet. Come on, let's look."

As they walked up the stairs, every step creaked. "Are you *really* going to buy this house?" Benny asked.

They went through all four bedrooms. Two of them still held some furniture. Alice peered out of a window onto an overgrown garden. "You know, Joe," she said, "with some work this might be just right for us."

"I don't think this house is right for anyone," Benny said. "It's dirty and creaky and it smells funny, too."

Joe looked around again. "We'll have to think about this, Alice. I'm just not sure."

They all left the house, and the door squeaked loudly as Alice closed it. "I don't think *I'd* like to live here," Violet said. "It's creepy."

When Henry's foot went through the wood of one of the porch steps, they all laughed. "I said it needed some work," Alice said.

When the Alden family reached the front walk, they noticed an old, white-haired man cutting the hedges that separated his house from the one they'd just been in.

The old man sniffed and said, "Looking at the old Roth house?"

"What's a Roth house?" Benny asked.

The old man snorted. "Roth! Roth! That's the name of the man who built the house you just came out of."

"Oh!" Benny said.

"I'm Charles Farley," the white-haired man said. "I live here. Who are you?"

The Aldens introduced themselves one by one. "We're thinking of buying the Roth house," Alice said.

"Are you *really*?" Violet asked.

"Now, Alice," Joe said, nervously, "we have to talk about that."

"If I were you young people, I'd *never* buy that old place. *Never!* Take my word for it," Mr. Farley said, firmly.

"I wouldn't buy it either," Benny said.

Alice walked closer to Mr. Farley. "Why would you never buy it. Do you think it's overpriced?"

Mr. Farley snorted again. "Who cares about the price? I wouldn't buy it because it's *haunted*."

"*Haunted!*" the Alden children all said at the same time.

Alice Alden laughed. "That's silly. Haunted by what?"

Mr. Farley narrowed his eyes. "By a ghost, of course."

Henry didn't believe in ghosts, but he wanted to be polite. "Whose ghost is it?"

Benny was wide-eyed. "Yes. Whose ghost is it?"

Mr. Farley started trimming the hedge again. "It's the ghost of young Celia Roth. She lived in that house with her father until 1917. Her mother had died when Celia was a baby. Then Celia just disappeared. No one ever did find out what happened to her. Her father never spoke of her again."

"How old was she when she . . . disappeared?" Violet asked timidly.

"Seventeen," Mr. Farley said. "Just seventeen. And no one ever found her — "

Alice looked at Benny and Violet's faces and interrupted Mr. Farley. "We have to go now. Children, come along."

They all piled into Joe and Alice's station wagon and headed home. Alice silently drove the car for a while and then said, "Kids, you know there are no such things as ghosts, don't you?"

Joe agreed. "You all know that, of course."

"Of course we do," Jessie said.

"Of course," Henry said.

But Benny and Violet were silent.

Joe and Alice dropped the children at their home. Joe said, "We're going on to Pine Grove. We have some big decisions to make. But first we'll stop by and give the key to the Roth house back to Mrs. Thaler, the real estate agent."

That night at dinner, the children told Grandfather about their visit to the Roth house. Henry was helping Mrs. McGregor carry a platter of chicken and bowls of little potatoes and peas in from the kitchen.

He took his seat at the table and said, "Can you imagine anything sillier than thinking a house is haunted?"

Grandfather laughed. "Well, of course it's silly, but I hope you were polite to Mr. Farley."

Benny looked at his grandfather. "You mean it? There really are no ghosts *anywhere*?"

Mr. Alden reached over and patted Benny's hand. "I really mean it," he said. "I hope you're not frightened."

"Not me!" Benny said firmly.

"Not me," Violet agreed.

The children all felt safe with Grandfather. They could hardly believe they had once run away from him. After their parents had died, they had heard that their grandfather was a mean man who wouldn't be nice to them. They had lived in a boxcar, until Mr. Alden had found them and took them and their boxcar back to his estate. Now the children couldn't be happier, and they loved their grandfather dearly.

When Mrs. McGregor brought in a big chocolate cake for dessert, Benny said, "I feel sorry for the ghosts. They'll never get to eat one of Mrs. McGregor's cakes. I think I'll eat an extra piece for them."

Mrs. McGregor sliced the cake and put two pieces on Benny's plate. "There you are, Benny," she said.

Just as they were all eating the cake, the phone rang. "I'll get it," Mr. Alden said and he walked into his study. He was on the phone for about five minutes before he returned to the dining room.

"Well, that was Joe. They've decided to buy that old house and move to Greenfield. They've already spoken to Mrs. Thaler, the agent," Grandfather said.

"The haunted one?" Benny asked.

"Come on, Benny. You know it isn't haunted," Mr. Alden said. "Aren't you happy Alice and Joe will be living here?"

Benny thought for a minute. "Yes, I am, but I'll miss going to the amusement park that's near where they live now."

"Well," Mr. Alden said, "I'll certainly be glad to have them here."

"When will they move in?" Jessie asked.

"Soon," Grandfather said. "I'm going to ask my lawyer to move things along quickly. They'd like to be settled in a couple of weeks."

"That place certainly needs a lot of work," Mrs. McGregor said as she brought in a bowl of fruit.

Jessie said, "Maybe *we* can fix it up a little."

Violet jumped up from the table. "What a wonderful idea! We could dust and clean out the closets and drawers. I noticed there were still things in some of them."

"We can oil the doors and windows," Henry said.

"And weed the garden," Benny added.

"And touch up some of the paint," Jessie said.

"I think Joe and Alice will be very happy to have you do all that," Grandfather said. "I'll pay for whatever supplies you need, of course."

"We'll need the key to get into the house," Henry said.

Mr. Alden nodded. "I'll call Mrs. Thaler in the morning and tell her to give you children the key."

"Can we take Watch?" Benny asked, looking at the Alden's dog, who was dozing in a corner.

Everybody laughed. "I don't think Watch would be much help," Grandfather said. "You'd better leave him at home."

"We'll take Watch some other time, Benny," Henry added, seeing Benny's disappointment.

Benny sighed. "I guess he'd have more fun at home anyway."

CHAPTER 2

Work! Work! Work!

The next morning, the Aldens got up and fixed a breakfast of orange juice, cold cereal, toast with strawberry jam, and milk. When they had eaten and cleaned up the kitchen, they ran down to the box-car.

It was almost the same as when they had lived in it. The only new things were the plump cushions Mrs. McGregor had made for the children to sit on. Now they made themselves comfortable on the pillows.

Benny pulled an apple out of his pocket and bit into it.

"Benny," Henry asked, "don't you ever stop eating?"

Benny grinned. "Yes — when I sleep."

"Okay," Jessie said, "let's make a list of everything we need to take to the old house."

"Well," Violet said, thoughtfully, "we need soap and rags and a mop . . ."

"And oil and paint and a paintbrush," Henry added.

"And, work gloves, and a broom and paper to line the drawers," Jessie said.

"And food," Benny said. "For us!"

"Okay," Jessie said. "We'll bike into town, buy all the stuff at the hardware store, and then we'll go to the market and get food for lunch. And then we can go to the 'Roth house,' as Mr. Farley calls it."

Henry said, "That's fine! Let's get our bikes and go."

Five minutes later the Aldens were biking down a tree-lined country road to the town of Greenfield. Once they reached the small town, they stopped at Mrs. Thaler's for the keys to the house. She handed Jessie two keys on a ring. "The larger one is for the front door and the smaller one is for the back door," she told them.

Then they rode over to Harmon's Hardware store. Mr. Harmon greeted them when they walked in. "Hi, Aldens. Can I help you?"

"We need a lot of cleaning things to take to the Roth house, which our cousins Joe and Alice are buying. We're going to help fix it up for them," Benny said all in one breath.

Mr. Harmon laughed. "It will take an army to fix that place up . . . *and* get rid of the ghosts."

Benny and Violet exchanged looks. "Ghosts?" they said together.

"Come on, Mr. Harmon," Jessie said. "Don't joke like that."

Mr. Harmon glanced at Benny's pale face. "Sure! Sure! I'm just joking. Now what can I get you?"

Henry handed Mr. Harmon the list. Mr.

Harmon looked at it and said, "That's quite a load. Tell you what — I have a delivery out that way this afternoon. I'll drop all this stuff off at the Roth place for you . . . around one o'clock."

"Great!" Jessie said. "Thanks a lot."

"I'll just put it all on your grandfather's account," Mr. Harmon said.

Benny said, "Now we can go to the store for our lunch food."

The Aldens walked across the street to a small market. Henry took a shopping cart, and the four children walked through the aisles. Into the cart they put a loaf of whole wheat bread, a large package of cheese slices, juicy tomatoes, peaches, chocolate cookies, and two quarts of milk. Benny added potato chips, and Violet ran back for paper plates, cups, and plastic tableware.

After they had paid, they divided the food into two bags. Henry and Jessie each put one in their bike baskets. Then they all rode the couple of miles to the old house. As they got off their bikes, a middle-aged man and

woman were getting into a car parked in the street. The dark-haired woman stared at the Aldens and then walked over to them.

"We're the Aldens," Benny said quickly. "Our cousins Joe and Alice are buying this house." He carefully pointed to the Roth house.

"I'm Gloria Carter," the woman said. "I live next door to the Roth house."

The man came over to her and she introduced him. "This is my husband, David." She turned to Mr. Carter. "Dave, the Roth house has been sold to the children's cousins."

Mr. Carter slowly narrowed his eyes. "I don't need any neighbors," he said gruffly.

Gloria Carter put her hand on her husband's arm and said, "Now, David, it will be lovely to have new young neighbors. I'm delighted!" She smiled. "We're driving into Greenfield to shop now. Will you be here long?"

"We're going to start cleaning up," Jessie

said. "We'll be here a lot in the next few weeks."

"How nice," Mrs. Carter said. "Then I'll see you again." The Carters got into their car and drove off.

The Aldens took the bundles from the bike baskets and carried them up to the porch. Jessie unlocked the door and they went into the house. "She was a nice lady," Benny said.

"Yes," Violet said. "But *he* wasn't very friendly."

Henry laughed. "Oh, well, one friendly neighbor out of two is okay."

Inside the house Benny wrinkled his nose. "Like I said before, it smells."

Henry went to a window and pulled it up. "It's just a little stuffy. Let's open *all* the windows. Upstairs, too. That will help."

"I'll go upstairs with you, Violet," Jessie said. "Benny, you stay down here and help Henry."

Upstairs, the girls went into each room and

pulled the windows up. Jessie looked into the largest bedroom. "Look, Violet, there are still shades on these windows."

Violet shook her head. "Yes, and look at them. They're torn and dirty and faded. I wonder if these are the Roth's shades, or if anyone lived in this house after they moved out."

"We can ask someone," Jessie said. "Let's go downstairs and see where we should begin to clean."

The girls ran lightly down the stairs and joined their brothers, who were in the living room. "Where should we start?" Jessie asked.

"We can't start anywhere," Benny said. "We have no cleaning things."

Jessie laughed. "Oh, I forgot. You *are* smart, Benny."

Benny grinned. "Well, then, I'm smart enough to know since we can't clean, we can at least eat. Let's fix lunch."

Henry shrugged and began to laugh. "We might as well."

Suddenly there was a loud *bang* from upstairs. The Aldens all jumped. "What was *that*?" Benny asked, his eyes wide.

Violet moved closer to Jessie. "There's nobody here but us — is there?" she asked, her voice shaking.

"I don't know, but I'll go look," Jessie said bravely.

"I'll go with you," Henry said.

Henry and Jessie walked up the stairs slowly. "What do you suppose it was?" Henry whispered to Jessie. He took her hand and they went from room to room.

In the large bedroom a shade was lying on the floor. Jessie laughed. "*That's* what it was. That shade fell off the window. The wind must have done it."

Henry sighed with relief. "All this ghost talk. You know it gets to you."

"Are you all right?" Violet called from downstairs.

"We're fine," Henry called back. "A window shade fell on the floor. That's all."

"Good," Benny called out. "Let's eat."

The Aldens went into the kitchen and unpacked their food. "How come there are lights and water, if no one lives here?" Benny asked.

"Real estate agents often turn them on when they know they are going to be showing a house," Henry said. "Joe told me that."

The children made sandwiches of cheese and tomatoes and put them on the paper plates. Benny opened the chips and Violet passed around the fruit and cookies. After Henry poured the milk they sat on the floor in the kitchen and ate.

While they were eating there was a knock at the back door. "Harmon's," a voice called out. The delivery boy from the hardware store brought the boxes of cleaning things into the kitchen and put them on the floor. He glanced around the grimy room and said, "Boy, you sure have a lot of work to do." Then he left.

When the Aldens had finished eating, they put all the garbage into a paper bag. "I wonder if there's a garbage can around here," Jessie asked. She looked around the kitchen.

"What's behind that door?" Benny asked, pointing to a heavy wooden door next to the sink.

"I don't know — I didn't even notice it until now," Jessie said.

She pulled open the door and peered into the darkness. "No garbage can. But there's a staircase going up. Who wants to come with me?"

First there was silence, then Benny said, "I'll go," but his voice was just a little shaky.

Slowly Benny and Jessie walked up the flight of stairs. It was very dark, and Benny hung onto Jessie's hand tightly. They came to another door at the top of the stairs and Jessie opened it. They were in one of the bedrooms. She laughed. "It just leads up to the second floor."

"I thought so," Benny said.

Jessie lightly poked his arm. "I'll bet," she said.

The Aldens spent the afternoon working. Henry and Jessie scrubbed the kitchen. Violet dusted the living room and dining room, and Benny weeded the garden. After a couple of hours, they all admitted they were tired.

"Let's go home," Benny said.

"Yes, let's," Violet agreed.

They neatened up the cleaning supplies, carefully locked the back door, and went out the front door. They locked that, too.

Mr. Farley was in his yard mowing the lawn. He stopped when he saw the Aldens come out. "What have you been doing?" he asked.

"Cleaning and weeding," Benny answered. "So when our cousins move in, they won't have as much work to do."

"So, they *are* buying it," Mr. Farley said. "Foolish people. There is never enough room in one house for real live people *and* a ghost."

"We don't believe in ghosts," Jessie said.

"You will," the old man answered. "When

you hear Celia Roth singing, you'll believe in ghosts."

"Did you know her . . . Celia?" Violet asked timidly.

"I did," Mr. Farley replied. "I was just a boy when she lived here, but I remember her well. She was a beautiful, sweet girl. Maybe you'll see her someday, when you're in the house."

"Mr. Farley," Henry said, "I don't think we will."

Mr. Farley laughed. "We'll see," he said.

CHAPTER 3

The Singing

When the children reached home, they all went into the den and sat down. "You know," Jessie said, "I wonder whether Mr. Farley is deliberately trying to scare us. He talks about the ghost so much."

"Why would he want to scare us?" Violet asked.

"I have no idea," Jessie replied. "I just wonder. It seems strange to me."

"He isn't very nice, if he's trying to scare children," Benny said.

"I can't think of any reason why he'd do that," Henry said.

Jessie sighed. "I guess you're right. But that would mean he really believes there is a ghost."

"Maybe there is," Benny said.

"No," Henry said, "that's impossible."

But Benny was not convinced.

The Aldens went back to the house the next morning determined not to think about ghosts.

Henry started painting the porch railings. Violet and Benny got scissors and paper to line the drawers in the kitchen.

Jessie went upstairs to dust away the cobwebs in the bedrooms. Out one of the windows Jessie caught a glimpse of a man standing across the street, staring up at the Roth house. She stepped away from the window so he couldn't see her, and then peeked out again. The man was still staring at the house.

Jessie ran down the stairs and went outside

to Henry. "Look at that man across the street," she said to her brother.

Henry stopped painting and gazed at the man. Even though now the two children were looking at him, the man never moved.

"Let's go talk to him," Jessie said.

"What can we say?" Henry asked.

Jessie grabbed Henry's hand. "Come on," she said.

They walked across the street and Jessie said to the man, "Hi. Can we help you? You've been standing here quite a while."

The man frowned. "What's happening to this house?" he asked gruffly.

Henry smiled. "Do you know the Roth house well?"

"I'm Thomas Yeats," the man said. "I'm an artist. I've been working on a large picture of the Roth house. It's going to be my finest painting. I've been working on it for months, but it's not finished yet. So no one can change the look of the house."

Henry said, "Our cousins are moving in

here in a few weeks. They may change the house quite a bit."

Tom Yeats's voice was cold. "They *can't*. They *can't* make all my hard work useless. I'll put a stop to that." His eyes were blazing with fury. He turned and swiftly walked away.

"Wow!" Jessie said. "He was angry."

Jessie and Henry went into the house and told Violet and Benny what had happened. "That Mr. Yeats was really mad," Henry said.

"If the house starts to look different, can't the man just paint another picture?" Benny asked.

Violet shook her head. "Artists aren't like that," she answered Benny. "If Mr. Yeats has worked hard on that painting for a long time, he wants to finish it, not start something new."

"He sure was upset," Jessie said, remembering the sound of Mr. Yeats's voice.

Benny got bored with Mr. Yeats. "I have a good idea," he said. "Let's eat lunch out on the porch. I'll get the food Mrs. McGregor fixed for us this morning."

"Good idea!" Henry said. "I'll help you."

The Aldens all went into the kitchen, got the picnic basket Mrs. McGregor had packed, and took it out onto the porch. Henry spread newspapers on the floor, and the children sat down. From the picnic basket they took paper plates and cups, turkey sandwiches, purple plums, cookies, and a thermos of lemonade. They began to eat.

Suddenly they heard a voice coming from the house. Someone was singing! It was a girl, singing sweetly. The Aldens all stopped eating and listened. The voice was louder now, coming from upstairs. Henry jumped up and went to the door, and the others followed him.

"Who is it?" Benny asked, his voice quivering.

"Mr. Farley talked about Celia Roth singing," Violet said, moving closer to Jessie. Her eyes were wide.

"That *can't* be!" Jessie said.

"But *who* is singing?" Henry asked.

As suddenly as it had started, the singing stopped. Benny breathed a sigh of relief.

"I'm going to see what's going on," Henry said, heading toward the stairs.

"I'll go, too," Jessie said.

"I'm not staying here alone," Benny whispered.

"Me either," Violet added.

So all four Aldens went upstairs and tiptoed from room to room.

"There's nothing here," Jessie said.

"It must have been a radio," Henry said.

"But there isn't a radio in the house," Violet pointed out.

"And who turned it on if there was one?" Benny asked.

The Aldens were silent. There didn't seem to be any answers to the questions.

"Let's go home," Benny said firmly.

Jessie looked at Benny and Violet's worried faces and said, "We did a lot this morning. I think we should leave the house until tomorrow."

"Good!" Benny said.

The Aldens walked back downstairs and onto the porch. They finished eating their lunch, though no one was very hungry. Then they began to clean up the porch. They stopped their work when Mrs. Carter came up the walk.

"I just thought I'd see if I could help you," she said, smiling.

"We're just leaving," Jessie replied. "But thank you."

Mrs. Carter stared at the house with a funny expression on her face. "Mr. Carter and I would have bought this place and the property, but we couldn't afford it. I guess your cousins could." She looked longingly at the house.

"What does 'afford' mean?" Benny asked.

"It means having enough money to buy something," Mrs. Carter answered. "I envy your cousins."

Violet felt sorry for Mrs. Carter and a little unhappy. "I'm sorry, Mrs. Carter. But you'll like Joe and Alice."

Mrs. Carter smiled now. "Don't let me keep you. You seemed to be packing up. Knock on my door if I can help you anytime." She left.

The Aldens watched her walk away. Then Benny said, "Maybe she was the lady singing."

Jessie smiled. "Benny, she wasn't in the house. It couldn't have been Mrs. Carter."

Benny looked disappointed.

Henry said reassuringly, "It was probably a radio turned on somewhere. There are houses all around us. It just *sounded* as if it was coming from upstairs."

That night after everyone was in bed, Henry knocked on Jessie's door. She called out, "Come in."

Henry sat down on Jessie's bed. She looked up from her book.

"Jessie, things are sure funny at the Roth house," Henry said.

"*You* don't believe there's a ghost, do you?" she asked.

"Of course not," Henry said. "But something is going on. Mr. Farley keeps talking about ghosts. Mr. Carter doesn't want neighbors. Mr. Yeats is angry. Shades fall off windows. A girl is singing in the house, when there is no girl there."

Jessie thought for a minute. "None of what you said means anything is wrong. I'm sure all those things can be explained."

"But how?" Henry asked.

"I don't know," Jessie said. "But we'll figure it out. We always do."

Henry nodded. "I guess you're right." He smiled. " 'Night, Jessie."

After Henry left, Jessie sat very still and thought, Henry is right. Something *is* funny at the Roth house.

CHAPTER 4

The Argument

In the morning none of the Aldens felt like going right to the house.

Benny said, "Can't we go somewhere else first? We can clean in the afternoon."

"Benny's right," Violet said.

Jessie thought for a minute and then said, "I know. Let's go to the lake in the park. We can swim and then go to the house."

"Great!" Henry agreed.

"I think we should stop at the bakery first and buy some jelly doughnuts," Benny said.

Henry laughed. "Okay, Benny, we can do that."

The children biked into town and went to the bakery. Joan Bernstein, a tall, blonde woman who owned the shop, smiled when the Aldens came in. She looked away from the customer she was waiting on and said, "Hi, Aldens. I'll be with you in a minute."

She finished putting chocolate cookies into a bag and then said, "I think you children should meet Terry Evans." She gestured toward her customer, who was a short red-haired woman. "Ms. Evans is writing a book about the history of Greenfield."

"Is Greenfield that important?" Benny asked.

Ms. Bernstein nodded. "This town goes way back to colonial times."

Terry Evans smiled at the Aldens. "Have you all lived here very long?" she asked them.

"Since our grandfather found us and brought us here," Benny answered.

Ms. Evans laughed and started to leave the store.

"The Aldens' cousins have bought that old Roth house," Ms. Bernstein said. "The children are cleaning it up for them. Everyone in town is talking about how helpful the kids are."

Terry Evans turned to the Aldens. "Oh," she said. "I hear that's a very interesting house. Can you tell me about it?"

"We don't know that much," Jessie said hesitantly.

"You must know something," Ms. Evans insisted.

"Just that Mr. Farley says it's haunted," Benny said.

"But we know that's silly, of course," Henry added.

"Is it?" Ms. Evans asked. She looked at the children mysteriously. Then she said, "I have to go now, but I'd like to talk to you all again." Then she left.

Benny looked after her. "She liked us, I think. She wants to talk to us again."

"Yes, but why?" Henry asked. "We told her we don't know much about the house."

"She's just a very curious woman," Joan Bernstein said. "Now, what can I give you children?"

"Jelly doughnuts," Benny answered. "We're going to take them to the park."

Violet got four small containers of orange juice from the cooler, and Ms. Bernstein put the doughnuts, juice, and straws into a bag. The Aldens paid her and went out to their bikes. "Be careful at the lake," she called after them.

"We will," Violet called back.

When they reached the park, they sat on the grass under a tree. The shimmering lake was only a few yards from them.

Benny opened the paper bag and gave his brother and sisters a doughnut. Violet passed around the juice and straws. They sat contentedly and ate their snack, watching three teenagers playing in the lake.

They waited a little while after they had finished eating. Then they stripped down to the bathing suits they had on under their clothes. They ran to the lake and swam and splashed. Benny stayed near the shore. The Aldens kept their eyes on each other while they swam.

When they finally ran out of the water, they dried themselves and lay on the grass, talking softly. Suddenly, very close by, they heard loud voices. Under a nearby tree were Mr. Farley and Thomas Yeats. They hadn't seen the Aldens.

"I'll never do that. *Never!*" Mr. Farley cried out.

"I'm willing to pay you," Thomas Yeats said.

"No! It's not about money. I won't do it," Mr. Farley insisted.

"Forget it!" Mr. Yeats said, and he strode away. In a few seconds Mr. Farley left, too.

"Wow!" Violet said.

"What was that all about?" Jessie asked.

"What do you suppose Mr. Yeats wanted Mr. Farley to do?" Henry asked.

"Whatever it was, he was willing to pay for it," Violet said.

"Mr. Farley was certainly definite," Jessie said.

"It's a mystery!" Benny said, smiling.

"It sure is," Violet agreed.

When the Aldens got to the house later that day, Terry Evans was sitting on a porch step. "I just wanted to ask you a few questions," she said.

"Oh," Jessie said. "What kind of questions?"

"About the house, of course," Terry replied. "Do you know anything about the girl who used to live here . . . Celia Roth?"

"The girl who disappeared?" Benny asked eagerly.

Terry nodded.

"We don't know anything at all," Violet answered.

"This house should really be a Greenfield landmark," Ms. Evans said. "With its strange history, no one should be allowed to buy it."

"What history?" Benny asked.

"Well," Terry said, "I've heard a number of people lived here after the Roths left. But no one stayed long. For whatever reasons, they left fairly quickly. Ghosts, you know." She smiled slyly, waved, and left.

Mr. Farley, who was back in his yard, walked over to the Aldens. "Why's that woman snooping around?" he asked. "She sure asks a lot of questions."

Henry wanted to ask Mr. Farley what he and Mr. Yeats had been arguing about. But he didn't want Mr. Farley to think they'd been eavesdropping. Instead he asked, "Mr. Farley, how long did Mr. Roth stay after Celia disappeared?"

Mr. Farley thought for a minute. "Just a few months. He was mysterious. Wouldn't talk about Celia at all. He just left Greenfield."

"Ms. Evans said other people lived here," Jessie said.

Mr. Farley nodded. "Yes, a few families bought the house, lived here a short time, and then left. It's been empty now for a good twenty years. The only thing left from the Roths is an old bed, that big old desk upstairs, and some boxes of old books."

"When did Celia disappear?" Jessie asked.

Mr. Farley said, "I remember it all well. I was only ten years old, but some things you don't forget. It was the summer of 1917. August, it was. A hot day in August and, poof, she just vanished. But I know she came back . . . to the house . . . for some reason . . . or at least her ghost did."

Henry laughed. "Come on, Mr. Farley. We just don't believe that."

The Aldens went into the house and sat down on the floor.

"What do you think happened to Celia?" Jessie asked.

"Maybe she was kidnapped," Violet said.

"Or she might have drowned in the lake," Henry suggested.

"Maybe Celia ran away, just like we did," Benny said.

"Yes, Benny, but Grandfather found us," Violet said. "No one ever found Celia."

CHAPTER 5

The Mysterious Dress

Suddenly, Benny sniffed. "I smell something sweet . . . like perfume."

"I smell it, too," Jessie said.

"It's like roses," Henry said.

"It's coming from the living room," Violet said.

The children hurried into the living room. There they saw something they didn't expect. On the mantel was a vase with three fragrant yellow roses in it.

"These weren't here yesterday," Violet said, startled.

"Maybe Mr. Farley took some from his garden and put them in here," Jessie said thoughtfully.

"Maybe, but how would he have gotten in? We always lock the door when we go," Henry said. "Let's go ask him."

The Aldens went outside. Mr. Farley was still working in his yard.

"Mr. Farley," Benny called out.

Mr. Farley stopped weeding as the children approached. "Yes?" he said.

"Did you put any roses in the living room in the Roth house?" Violet asked.

Mr. Farley snorted. "Of course not. I don't grow roses, and I sure wouldn't waste money buying flowers for an empty house."

"Well, someone did," Jessie said. "Come look."

Mr. Farley followed the Aldens into the house and into the living room. He looked at the roses on the mantel. "Well, you're right. They sure are roses."

"Maybe Mrs. Carter put them here," Henry said.

"She and her husband went off early this morning," Mr. Farley said, "and they haven't come home yet."

The Aldens were silent.

"I told you there were funny things going on in this house. Now maybe you'll believe me," Mr. Farley said. "Celia used to love roses. I remember that. She grew them in her garden." Then he turned and went back to his house.

"Mr. Farley is right. There are strange things going on," Violet said.

"Violet, there are good explanations for everything," Jessie said, but she didn't sound too sure.

"I know what we should do," Henry said. "We'll go to the library in the morning and see what we can find out about the Roths from old newspapers."

"Great idea," Jessie said.

"I think we should tell Grandfather what's going on," Benny said.

"Benny is right," Violet said.

Jessie hesitated. "We don't want him to think we're just foolish kids."

Henry shook his head. "Grandfather would never think that. He knows we aren't."

At the table that night, they all ate Mrs. McGregor's delicious meal of lamb chops, baked potatoes, and string beans. Then she brought in a big bowl of cut-up fresh fruit and a plate of spice cookies. She put the bowl in front of Henry to serve. As he dished out the fruit for his family, he said, "Grandfather, there's something we want to talk to you about."

Grandfather looked concerned. "There's nothing wrong, is there?"

"It's about the Roth house," Benny said. "It's a funny house."

"Funny?" Grandfather asked.

"Well," Violet began. "Benny is right. There are funny things *in* the house and funny people *outside* the house."

Jessie said, "The things in the house can all be explained, I'm sure. Like a window shade suddenly fell on the floor. And we heard a girl singing upstairs. And roses appeared in the living room. The shade was probably blown off the window by the wind. Henry thinks the singing came from outside the house. I guess someone put the roses in the house, but who?"

Grandfather smiled. "Probably Mrs. Thaler did, to make the house look pretty."

"I never thought of her," Violet said. "But what about the funny people?"

"How are they funny?" Mr. Alden asked.

Benny said, "Well, Mr. Farley, the next-door neighbor, is always saying the house is haunted."

Violet added, "And the other neighbor, Mr. Carter, doesn't want to *have* neighbors."

Henry said, "And there's this man, an artist named Thomas Yeats, who is upset because the house will be fixed up. He's painting a picture and doesn't want the house changed."

"And there's Terry Evans. She's writing a book. *She* thinks the house should be a landmark," Jessie said.

"These people don't sound so odd to me, except maybe Mr. Farley," Grandfather said. "But he probably just has a big imagination. I think you children do, too. I suggest you forget about Mr. Farley's ghost and have fun fixing up the house. Joe and Alice will be so pleased."

"You're right, Grandfather," Jessie said. "That's just what we'll do. We all do have *big* imaginations."

But in the morning, the Aldens went to the library anyway. Ms. Gary, the librarian, smiled at them. "Can I help you?" she asked.

Jessie smiled back at her. "We wonder if you have any old Greenfield newspapers that go back to 1917?"

"We have some on microfilm. Is there anything in particular you're looking for?" Ms. Gary asked.

"Well, we'd like to read about when Celia Roth disappeared. Our cousins are buying the old Roth house," Violet said.

"That was a long time ago," Ms. Gary said.

"It was August," Benny said. "Mr. Farley told us that."

"Well, that's a help," Ms. Gary said as she left the room. "I'll be right back."

She returned soon with two rolls of microfilm. "This is the Greenfield paper from August 1917. Do you know how to use the microfilm machine?" she asked. "It's upstairs."

"I know how. We learned in school," Jessie said.

"Ours is an old machine," Ms. Gary said. "Not like the newest ones."

"So is the one in school," Jessie replied. The Aldens ran up the stairs, and Jessie put the film into the machine and started moving the film through. "I'll yell when I get to something," she said, looking at the screen.

The other children were silent while Jessie looked. After a while she shouted, "Here! Here's something."

"Let me see," Violet said. "The date is August 4th. It says, *Celia Roth is missing*."

"What else does it say?" Benny asked excitedly.

Violet read. "*Seventeen-year-old Celia Roth has vanished from her father's house. Mr. Robert Roth has refused to discuss the disappearance with reporters. The Greenfield police have questioned Mr. Roth and they also refuse to be interviewed*."

"Let me look, too," Henry said. He took Violet's place at the machine. "Here's more. On August thirty-first it says, *The Greenfield police are no longer investigating the case of Celia Roth*."

"That's funny," Jessie said. "Keep looking."

Henry looked for another five minutes. "There's nothing else," he said.

The Aldens went downstairs, returned the film to Ms. Gary, and left the library.

Benny said, "Well, we don't know anything more than we did before."

They all got on their bikes. "Let's go to the house and do some more work," Jessie said. "Before we know it, Joe and Alice will be here."

When they got to the house, Thomas Yeats was across the street. His easel was set up and he was busy working on his painting of the Roth house.

Benny waved and called out, "Hi, Mr. Yeats. Can I look at your painting?"

Mr. Yeats looked across the street at Benny. "No, you can't," he replied gruffly.

"It's probably a rotten painting anyway," Benny grumbled.

"He sure is an unfriendly man," Jessie said.

"Let's just ignore him," Violet said. "I know what needs cleaning very badly . . .

the big bathroom in the master bedroom."

"Ugh," Benny said. "I don't want to clean a bathroom."

"Okay, Benny," Henry said, "you can clean the inside of the big bedroom's windows. I'll help Jessie and Violet with the bathroom."

The Aldens carted cleanser, soap, a bucket, and rags up to the bathroom. Jessie and Violet scrubbed the sink and the tub while Henry washed down the tiles. Little by little the bathroom began to look white instead of gray.

In the bedroom, Benny sprayed window cleaner on the panes of glass and carefully wiped them with a soft rag. The sun sparkled on the panes and Benny cried out, "You should see what a good job I'm doing!"

"I'm sure you are," Violet called back to Benny. "We'll come and look."

The Aldens gathered around Benny and admired his hard work. Then Jessie pointed to a closet door. "We never looked in there."

Henry walked over and pulled open the heavy wooden door. He peered into the closet. "There are a few boxes in here."

The other children came over to him and looked into the closet, too. Violet said, "There are books in those boxes. Lots of books."

"We'll have to go through them some time," Jessie said. "That should be fun."

"Like when we cleaned up that old library," Benny said.

"Maybe there are boxes of things in the other closets," Violet said. "I'll go look in the next bedroom."

In a few minutes the children heard her cry out, "Come here! Look what's on the bed."

Benny, Henry, and Jessie ran into the next room. Violet pointed to the single bed that was against a wall and stretching into the room. What they saw surprised them even more than the roses had. There was a dress on the bed. A pale pink, long dress. The hem, neckline, and wrists were trimmed with a delicate lace. It was a beautiful dress, and the children could tell that it was very old.

"That dress wasn't here yesterday," Violet said.

"It wasn't here any day we were in this room," Henry added.

"Where do you suppose it came from?" Jessie asked.

"I'll bet it was once Celia's dress," Benny said.

"It looks like it might have been. And I'll bet this was her room," Violet said.

The Aldens were silent, each thinking about how the dress could have gotten into the room.

"I'm going to call Grandfather," Violet said. "I want him to come here and see what we see. Then he won't think we just have big imaginations."

"There's no phone in this house," Benny said. "How are you going to call him?"

"I'll go next door and ask the Carters if I can use their phone. I know they're home because I saw their car in the driveway," Violet said firmly.

"I don't know if we should bother Grandfather at work with this," Jessie said thoughtfully.

"Grandfather won't mind," Benny said. "He always tells us we should call him anytime if we need him."

Henry said, "That's true, but do we really need him to come to look at an old dress?"

"It isn't just an old dress, Henry," Violet said. "You know that. It's a *very old dress* that just suddenly appeared out of *nowhere*. I want Grandfather to see it."

"Okay," Jessie said. "Let's go and call him."

The Aldens hurried next door to the Carter's house and knocked at the door. Soon Mrs. Carter appeared. She smiled when she saw the children. "Hi. Can I do something for you?"

"We'd like to use your phone, if we could," Violet said. "I want to call my grandfather."

"I hope nothing is wrong," Mrs. Carter said, looking very curious.

"Well, I'm not sure," Violet replied. "Something very strange just happened to us."

"Do you want to tell me about it?" Mrs. Carter asked.

"First I want to call Grandfather," Violet said.

Mrs. Carter led the Aldens into the house. "There's a phone in the kitchen that you can use," she said, pointing to a room to her right.

Violet took the receiver off the kitchen wall and dialed a number. "I'd like to speak to Mr. Alden, please," she said. "This is his granddaughter Violet."

Soon Mr. Alden's voice boomed over the phone. "Violet! Are you all right? Is something wrong?"

"We're fine, Grandfather," she said.

"Don't be upset. But something just happened at the Roth house, and I'd like you to come over. A dress appeared, an old dress, out of nowhere."

Grandfather hesitated. "I'm sure there's a logical explanation, dear. But you do sound upset. I'll be with you as soon as I can drive over there."

Violet hung up. Mrs. Carter was leaning against the sink, looking very interested in Violet's conversation. The other Aldens were standing near the doorway.

"How about if I give you children some milk and cookies while you're waiting for your grandfather?" Mrs. Carter said.

"I think that's a very good idea," Benny said.

"Are you sure it isn't any trouble?" Jessie asked.

"It will be a pleasure," Mrs. Carter answered.

Just then Mr. Carter came into the kitchen. "I thought I heard a lot of strange voices," he said.

Mrs. Carter looked at him with a funny expression on her face. "It's just the Alden children. They're going to have milk and cookies while they wait for their grandfather."

"Why is *he* coming?" Mr. Carter asked. "Aren't there enough people here?"

Mrs. Carter laughed nervously. "Don't mind my husband, children. He really isn't as grumpy as he sounds."

She opened the refrigerator door and took out a large carton of milk. She filled four glasses and set them on the kitchen table. "Sit down. I'll put out some cookies, too."

The Aldens sat around the table, and Mr. Carter left the room. Mrs. Carter filled a plate with chocolate chip cookies and placed it in the center of the table. "They aren't homemade but they are still good," she said, smiling.

The Aldens drank and ate in silence. Then Benny slowly said, "Did you know Celia Roth?"

Mrs. Carter laughed. "No. She lived here way before I did. But I've certainly heard a lot about her from Mr. Farley."

"Do you believe in ghosts, Mrs. Carter?" Benny asked.

"Of course she doesn't," Henry said quickly.

CHAPTER 6

The Diary

Soon the Aldens heard a car stop in front of the Roth house. They ran to the front door and saw Mr. Alden getting out of the car.

"There's our grandfather," Jessie said to Mrs. Carter. "We have to go. Thanks for the phone and the snack."

"Any time," Mrs. Carter replied.

The children ran to their grandfather, and Violet said, "Come upstairs and see the dress I was telling you about."

They all went into the house and upstairs to the small bedroom. They looked at the bed. It was empty.

"The dress was here just a little while ago," Violet cried out. "Everyone saw it. We all did."

"She's right, Grandfather," Henry said. "It *was* here."

"We *all* saw it," Jessie added.

"It was right here on the bed?" Grandfather asked.

"Yes!" Violet said. "I can't believe it's gone."

"That is very odd," Mr. Alden said. He looked around the room thoughtfully. "There must be a good explanation. Meanwhile, I hope you children aren't nervous here."

"Of course not, Grandfather," Jessie said. "It *is* funny that the dress is gone. But there must be a real good reason."

"Something else happened," Henry said. "We found a couple of boxes of old books in a closet."

"That sounds interesting," Mr. Alden said. "Let me see them."

They walked into the master bedroom and showed Grandfather the books in the closet. He started looking through one box. "It's much too dark in this closet to see anything. I think we should take the boxes home and see what's in them. There might be something valuable."

"I'll help you carry the boxes downstairs," Henry said.

Together Henry and Mr. Alden carried the two boxes down and put them in Mr. Alden's car. "I think you children have had enough for one day. Why don't you bike home now," he said.

"I like that idea," Benny replied.

"Before we go, Grandfather. Look at the man across the street. He's the artist we told you about," Violet said.

Mr. Alden gazed at Thomas Yeats. "He seems ordinary enough to me, Violet. Just an artist painting a picture of a house."

"Not a very nice artist," Violet said. "A

grumpy one, just like Mr. Carter."

Grandfather laughed. "Well, unfortunately, everyone isn't pleasant all the time."

It took much longer for the children to bike home than for Mr. Alden to drive there. So by the time they had arrived at their house, Grandfather already had the boxes of books in the den. He also had some good news for them.

He said, "Aunt Jane called. Uncle Andy is away on business, so she's going to come and spend a few days visiting us."

Benny asked, "When will she get here? I can't wait."

Grandfather laughed. "Well, you won't have to wait too long. She'll be here in the morning. She said she would leave Elmford very early."

Violet was already busy pulling books out of the two cartons. The other children joined her and they all sat on the floor, examining them. Grandfather sat in his favorite chair reading the newspaper. He enjoyed their laughter as they found books that seemed very old and outdated.

Jessie pulled out a magazine that featured women's styles. "Look at these dresses," she cried out. "They're so funny."

"And the hats," Violet added. "Can you imagine wearing something like that now?"

Henry looked at the pictures, too. "You know, some of these dresses look just like the one that was on the bed in the Roth house."

Jessie closed the magazine and looked at the date on the cover. "This is from February 1917."

"So the dress we saw *could* have been Celia's," Violet said softly.

"*Violet!*" Jessie said. "Even if it was Celia's dress a long time ago, there's no such thing as ghosts. The dress got on the bed in some logical way."

Mrs. McGregor came to the door of the den and said, "Dinner will be ready in five minutes. You children all go upstairs and wash your hands very well. You're all dirty from those dusty old books."

In a few minutes they all sat down to a wonderful chicken dinner. The children were impatient, however, to get back to the books, which interested them all. Even Benny had found something special — a few old children's books. And Watch liked sniffing at the old books. So they ate faster than usual and decided to save their dessert until later.

They ran back into the den and continued going through the two boxes. The evening was filled with one or another of the children calling out, "Look at this one" or "Have you ever seen anything like this?" or "Look at what a car looked like then!"

Suddenly Violet called out, "I've found something wonderful!"

She held in her hands a cracked blue leather book. Printed on the cover in gold letters was *My Diary*. On the first page was written in a delicate, perfect handwriting, *This book belongs to Celia Roth.*

The Aldens all crowded around Violet and looked at the diary. "I'm not sure it's right to read it," Jessie said.

"Jessie, the diary is years and years old. Celia Roth is probably dead now. What harm is there in reading it?" Violet asked.

Jessie said firmly, "I wouldn't want anyone reading *my* diary — even seventy-five years later."

Violet turned to Mr. Alden, who was listening to the conversation. "What do *you* think, Grandfather?"

Mr. Alden said, "Well, I don't really see anything wrong in reading the diary of someone who wrote it so long ago."

Violet opened the book, and Henry said, "See if there are any entries for August, the month she disappeared."

Violet read aloud: "*August 1, 1917 . . . Dear Diary, I told Father last night that I was in love with George Collins and that we wanted to get married. I explained that since George is in the army and due to go overseas we wanted to be wed before he went. Father was very upset. He said he would never allow that. He said George and I didn't know each other well enough and that it was a foolhardy thing to do. He said he would never give his permission. I cried and cried but he refused to change his mind."*

Jessie sighed. "Isn't that romantic?"

"Read some more, Violet," Henry said.

Violet went on. *"August 3, 1917 . . . Dear Diary, I tried to talk to Father about George again, but he still won't listen to how I feel. He wants George and me to wait until the end of the war. But who knows how long it will last? George is coming over tonight and he is going to try to change Father's mind.*

"August 4, 1917 . . . Dear Diary, George had no luck either. I am so unhappy. I don't want to disobey Father, but I want so much to marry George now.

"August 5, 1917 . . . Dear Diary, George and I had a long talk today. He is sure he is going to be shipped to Europe soon. What are we going to do? I never thought Father could be so stubborn. I know Father loves me and I love him. But I love George, too.

"*August 6, 1917 . . . Dear Diary, I feel much better tonight. Father seemed so calm and kind today. I am sure that if I'm patient he will come around and see my point of view. He almost always does. I'm sure everything will be fine.*"

Violet flicked the pages. "That's the last entry," she said.

Jessie frowned. "It seems as if Mr. Roth really didn't understand how unhappy Celia was."

Benny said, "I think it's all very mushy."

The other children laughed. Grandfather said, "Well, children, you certainly have made an interesting discovery. But now it's late. Benny, I think you should be off to bed."

Benny kissed Mr. Alden good night and started for the stairs. He smiled broadly. "Tomorrow Aunt Jane will be here."

CHAPTER 7

Aunt Jane Arrives

In the morning, the Aldens made breakfast. Jessie dipped pieces of bread into egg and milk for French toast. Benny set the table. Violet put out the maple syrup and jam, and Henry filled glasses with milk.

After the bread was browned, the children ate the tasty meal and then cleaned up the kitchen.

"Let's wait in the boxcar for Aunt Jane," Benny said.

Henry said, "Good idea. I'll tell Mrs. McGregor where we are."

Once the Aldens were in their beloved boxcar, they sat on the floor on the colorful cushions.

"You know," Jessie said, "before I went to sleep last night I kept thinking about the Roth house. I kept wondering if someone was deliberately trying to scare us away — and scare Joe and Alice away, too."

"What do you mean?" Henry asked.

"Well," Jessie went on, "maybe someone is behind the singing, and the dress, and all that . . . doing it on purpose."

"Who would want to do a thing like that?" Violet asked.

"I don't know for sure," Jessie answered, "but look at all the people who might have a reason. Mr. Carter doesn't want any neighbors. And Mr. Yeats doesn't want the house changed. And Ms. Evans thinks the house should be a landmark. Maybe one of them thinks we'll tell Joe and Alice not to buy the house."

"Yeah," Benny said, "and Mr. Farley is just plain weird."

Henry shook his head. "Jessie, no one has a key to the house but Joe and Alice, and now us. So how would someone get in? There has never been any sign of anyone breaking in."

"Henry is right," Violet said.

Jessie sighed. "I don't know."

Then Violet read to Benny while Jessie and Henry worked on a model airplane, until there was a knock at the door. Benny opened it, and there was Aunt Jane.

"It's so good to see all of you," she cried, hugging each one of them.

"We're awfully glad to see you, too," Violet said. "We have an extra pillow, so you can sit down with us."

When they all settled themselves on the pillows, Aunt Jane said, "Your grandfather tells me you've been having some mysterious adventures in Joe and Alice's new house."

"We certainly have," Violet said. And she

immediately started telling her aunt the entire story of the house and all the strange happenings. She also told her about Mr. Farley and the Carters and Thomas Yeats and Terry Evans.

"*And*," Jessie said, "we found Celia's diary yesterday."

Then they all had to tell Aunt Jane about the diary. She listened carefully and said, "There certainly has been a lot happening. I think we should go over to the house now and you can show me around."

They piled into Aunt Jane's car and rode into Greenfield. As they drove down Main Street, Violet cried out, "Look!"

"What?" Henry asked.

"It's Ms. Evans, and look at what she's carrying."

They all looked at Terry Evans, who was walking down the street. Her arms were full of yellow roses.

"Remember," Violet said, "we found three yellow roses in the living room at the Roth house. And *we* didn't put them there."

Aunt Jane laughed. "Violet, dear, anyone can buy yellow roses."

"Aunt Jane is right," Henry said.

"That's true," Violet said. "But it doesn't mean Ms. Evans *didn't* put the roses we saw into the living room."

When they got to the house, Aunt Jane went over to admire Mr. Farley's garden, as the children headed up to the porch. Benny pointed to the mailbox. "There's a letter in it," he said.

Jessie reached into the box and took out an envelope. On the front was printed THE ALDEN CHILDREN. She opened the envelope, took out a piece of paper, read it, and gasped.

"What does it say?" Henry asked.

Jessie handed the letter to Henry. He read, "*Aldens: Go home and stay home.*"

"I'll bet Mr. Carter wrote it. He said he didn't like neighbors," Benny said.

Henry said firmly, "We certainly aren't going to let whoever wrote it scare us away. Are we?"

"No!" Jessie said.

"We aren't," Benny agreed.

"I guess not," Violet said.

Henry looked back at Aunt Jane, who was coming up the front walk. "Don't mention this to Aunt Jane. She and Grandfather might not want us to come back here any-more — and then we'd never solve this mystery."

"That certainly is a beautiful garden next door," Aunt Jane said, stepping up onto the porch. "Come on, let's go in and you can give me a tour."

They all went through the house, and Aunt Jane said, "It's a lovely house. Joe and Alice will be very happy here. And you children have done a lot of cleaning. I can see that."

"But there is still more we want to do," Violet said. "We want to finish cleaning out the closets, and we haven't gone through the big desk."

"And I have a little more painting to do," Henry said.

"And I want to finish cleaning the windows," Benny added.

"Well," Aunt Jane said, "you still have time. Grandfather says Joe and Alice won't be here for another couple of weeks."

There was a knock on the door, and a telephone man came in. "I have an order for a phone to be installed here. A Mr. James Alden left it with the phone company."

"That's our grandfather," Benny said.

"Where do you want it?" the man asked.

Aunt Jane looked thoughtful. "Why don't you put it in the kitchen? Then the owners can have extensions added wherever they want them."

The telephone man went into the kitchen, and Aunt Jane and the children sat on the porch steps while he worked. Mrs. Carter saw them there and came over. The Aldens introduced her to Aunt Jane.

Mrs. Carter said, "Your nieces and nephews have certainly been busy fixing up this place. They don't even seem to be bothered by the rumors of a ghost in the house."

Aunt Jane smiled. "Of course they aren't bothered. They are sensible children and certainly don't believe in ghosts."

Just then the phone man came outside. "Well, I've hooked up the phone and it's working."

The man left and Aunt Jane asked, "Do you children want to stay here and work or not? I'm ready to go home."

Benny said, "I want to be with you, Aunt Jane."

"Me, too," the other Aldens said.

"Good," their aunt said. "We'll stop in town and have some lunch and then go home."

They ate in the Greenfield Coffee Shop and then spent the afternoon playing Monopoly and Scrabble with Aunt Jane. None of the children mentioned the nasty letter they'd received.

At the dinner table that night, Grandfather said, "I have some good news for you. Alice called this afternoon and said they are planning on moving earlier than they thought they would. They've sold their house and the new owners want to move in next week, if possible."

"Next week!" Jessie cried out. "We won't have time to finish everything."

"Well, just do the best you can," Mr. Alden said. "I know you've done a great deal already."

Henry sat silently. Then he said, "I have an idea! Suppose we go over tomorrow and stay overnight. That way we can work all day and the next morning, too, without going back and forth."

Benny looked surprised. "There's only one bed," he said.

"We'll bring sleeping bags," Jessie said.

"And food," Benny added.

Violet looked unsure. "You want to stay there *at night*?" she asked.

"Violet," Jessie said firmly, "there's nothing to be nervous about. You know there are *no ghosts* in that house."

"I forgot about the ghost," Benny said.

Grandfather looked uncertain. "I certainly don't think there are any ghosts in the house, but I'm not sure you children should stay there alone."

Jessie looked at Aunt Jane pleadingly. Aunt Jane said, "Well, James, there *are* neighbors on both sides of them. That Mrs. Carter seems like a very nice woman. If they needed anything I'm sure she would be very helpful."

"And the phone has been installed," Henry added. "So we can always call you."

Grandfather smiled. "It's hard to resist you children. I guess it's all right. But the least little thing that goes wrong, you will call me. Right?"

"Absolutely, Grandfather," Jessie said.

CHAPTER 8

The Letter

The next afternoon, the children packed up their sleeping bags, pajamas, and a change of clothes. Henry put in a flashlight, some more cleaning equipment, and a camera.

"What's the camera for?" Benny asked, sounding puzzled.

"I just thought it would be fun to take some pictures while we're working. Joe and Alice can put them in their scrapbook," Henry said.

Aunt Jane said, "I'll drive you all over to the house and pick you up in the morning."

"Can we take Watch?" Benny asked.

"That's a good idea," Henry said. "He's a good watch dog."

"What about food?" Benny asked.

"I heard that," Mrs. McGregor said. She came into the living room carrying a big picnic basket. "Everything you'll need is in here. For dinner there is a cold roast chicken, raw vegetables, potato salad, and cake. There's fresh fruit for an evening snack. Just remember to put everything in the refrigerator as soon as you get to the house."

"I'll remember that," Violet said.

"Oh," Mrs. McGregor said, "there are also two cartons of milk and a thermos of lemonade. And cold cereal and bananas for breakfast."

"They certainly won't starve." Aunt Jane laughed.

They all piled into Aunt Jane's car, and she drove to the Roth house. Watch jumped out when the door was opened and ran around the house. When Henry whistled, however, he came right back.

"You'd better keep him indoors," Aunt Jane said. "You don't want him to ge lost."

"Don't worry," Benny said. "He won't go far."

"All right," Aunt Jane said. "I'll be back in the morning. If you need anything, just call home."

The children watched her car drive away and then they went inside. They got to work right away, polishing and scrubbing and making sure the house was as clean as they could make it. As they worked, they noticed the sun that had filled the house was gone. Violet looked out of a window and said, "Look at the sky! It's filled with dark clouds."

Henry looked out, too. "It's going to rain. I'll turn on the radio and see what the weather report is."

The Aldens gathered around the radio and

listened. *"A severe storm watch is now in effect,"* the announcer said. *"Heavy rain and lightning are expected."*

Benny frowned. "I don't like that."

Henry laughed. "You're not afraid of thunder and lightning."

"I know," Benny said. "But I just hope the lights don't go out."

Violet's eyes widened. "Me, too."

Jessie said quickly, "Come on, let's get dinner ready. We can open our sleeping bags and sit on them while we eat."

The Aldens all went into the kitchen and took Mrs. McGregor's feast out of the refrigerator. They put everything on paper plates and sat on the living room floor to eat their dinner.

As they were finishing, a flash of brilliant lightning filled the room, followed by a loud clap of thunder. The lights flickered and the children all exchanged worried glances.

Something banged upstairs. "What was that?" Violet asked.

"It's probably just a door that blew shut," Jessie said.

"But there are no windows open to blow it shut," Violet said.

Watch sat next to Violet, his tail beating on the floor, and he whined loudly. "Even Watch is scared," Benny said.

"There's nothing to be scared of, Benny," Henry said.

Suddenly a sweet smell filled the room. The smell of roses. "There's that smell again. Like roses. Only there are no roses here," Violet said. "Remember they died and we threw them away."

"Well, then only the smell stayed," Jessie said.

"I want to talk to Grandfather," Benny said. "I just want to say hello."

"Go ahead, Benny," Henry said, following him into the kitchen.

Benny picked up the phone. "It's not working. There's no sound at all."

Henry took the phone out of Benny's hand. He listened, frowning. "Well, I guess the storm knocked some phone lines down. I'm sure it will be fixed soon."

Henry and Benny went back into the living room. "The phone isn't working," Henry said.

Violet gasped. The lights flickered again and then a sound came from upstairs. It was the same sweet voice they had heard before, singing the same sweet song. The Aldens sat in silence, scarcely breathing. And then, after a few minutes, the singing stopped.

"It can't be a radio this time," Violet said. "And all the windows are shut."

"Well, it has to be coming from somewhere," Henry said. "And it isn't from a ghost. It's just drifting in. We'll figure out from where. Meanwhile I say we get to work! There is a lot to do upstairs."

"Upstairs?" Benny said.

"Yes," Jessie agreed. "There is *nothing* up there to be afraid of, and if we do some work, it will take your mind off of the singing."

The children walked up the stairs. Jessie said, "There's that big desk in the one room we haven't looked at."

They went into the small room that held the big desk and Henry pulled open a drawer. It was filled with pads of blank paper. The Aldens opened every drawer and emptied them of old pencils, rubber bands, a pair of glasses, and assorted odds and ends. When they reached the next drawer, Henry pulled on it but it didn't move. Jessie pulled, too, and still the drawer remained shut.

"We'll never get this open," Henry said.

"Let me try once more," Jessie insisted.

She pulled as hard as she could and finally it flew open. Jessie peered inside. "There's an envelope stuck back here!" The envelope was stuck half in the drawer and half against the back of the desk. She took the drawer out of the desk, reached inside, and pulled out the envelope.

Jessie turned it over and said softly, "Look!"

Written on the front in a delicate, perfect handwriting was the word *Father*.

"It's Celia's handwriting," Violet said. "The same handwriting that was in the diary."

"Open it, Jessie!" Benny said.

Jessie ripped open the envelope and took out one sheet of paper that had the same delicate handwriting the children now could recognize.

"What does it say?" Henry asked.

Jessie said in a soft voice, "It's dated August 10, 1917. And it says:

Dear Father:

I have tried to obey you always, but now I just can't. I love George very much and we are going to be married. I am going to his parents' home in Bromley and we will be married there in a few days.

I don't mean to hurt you. Please call me when you read this and please come to our wedding.

I am putting this letter in this drawer be-

cause I know you open it every morning to take out your reading glasses to read the morning paper. So I know you will find the letter right away.

I love you very much and will be waiting to hear from you.

Your daughter, Celia"

The Aldens were silent. Then Violet said, "The letter must have gotten stuck in the back of the drawer, and Mr. Roth never saw it."

"So he thought that Celia had disappeared and he had no idea where she could have gone," Jessie said.

"Wow!" Benny said. "That was a real mystery."

Violet's voice trembled a little. "Poor Celia. She must have waited to hear from her father and she never did. So she thought he didn't want to talk to her."

"It's so sad," Jessie said.

Just then Benny let out a big yawn. Henry smiled at him. "Let's quickly finish cleaning out this desk, then we can go to sleep," he said. "It's been a long day."

The bottom drawer opened easily. Violet looked in and said, "Look at this! It's a tape player."

She lifted it out carefully and placed it on the desk.

"There's a tape in it, too," Benny said.

Jessie rewound the tape to where it started and pushed the play button. A girl's sweet voice, singing a sad song, filled the room. "That's the singing we've been hearing," Jessie cried out.

"*It was a tape all the time*," Violet said. "Not Celia's ghost."

"There's no such thing as *ghosts*, Violet," Benny said.

"This tape recorder couldn't have belonged to the Roths. It's brand-new," Jessie pointed out. "Someone brought it here just to play this tape."

"Who would do that?" Henry asked. "Who would play this, knowing it would bother us?"

"Let's go downstairs and get into our sleeping bags," Violet said. "We can talk about it some more."

Once the children were snugly in their sleeping bags, Jessie said, "Well, someone is deliberately trying to scare us. Who?"

"It's probably the same person who brought the flowers and the dress and left the letter in the mailbox," Henry said.

By now the rain had stopped and the house was quiet. "Can we talk about this in the morning?" Benny asked. "I'm sleepy."

Henry laughed. "Sure. But there isn't that much to talk about. It has to be either Mr. Carter or Mr. Farley or Ms. Evans or Mr. Yeats."

"But how do we find out which one of them it is?" asked Violet.

"I don't know," said Henry. "Maybe we'll think of something in the morning."

CHAPTER 9

The Back Stairs

The Aldens woke up early. The storm had moved on, and sun filled the house as they ate the breakfast of cold cereal and bananas and drank the milk Mrs. McGregor had packed. They tried the phone and were happy to find it was working again.

"There isn't much more work we can do," Violet said. "Let's just clean up the kitchen."

"I want to go upstairs again and make sure everything looks neat there," Jessie said.

"We can use the back staircase," Henry added.

The children walked up the back stairs, which Henry lit with the flashlight. Halfway up, Jessie stepped on something soft, and stumbled. She bent down and picked up a gray and red sweater. "This is Mrs. Carter's," she said. "She had it on the first time we met her. Why is it here?"

"She must have been using this staircase," Henry said.

"But how did she get in?" Violet asked. "We were always so careful to lock the doors."

"Then she must have had a key," Benny said. "But why does she have it?"

"I know what we should do," Jessie said. "We'll hide outside. If we close all the windows and pull down all the shades, the Carters will think we've gone home. If they're the ones who've been trying to scare us, they'll probably come back into the house again soon."

The Aldens quickly packed their things

and rolled up their sleeping bags. Henry looked out the window and spotted a couple of large bushes at the side of the house that would be a perfect hiding place. They were big enough for the children to hide in, and from there they'd be able to see anyone who might come up the front walk or use the back door.

The children locked up the house, and walked down the front walk as if they were going home. Then one by one they sneaked into the bushes. Jessie and Benny watched the front walk, and Henry and Violet watched the back door.

"Look!" Henry finally whispered. "Mr. and Mrs. Carter are going in the back door. And they *do* have a key."

The Aldens stayed hidden and soon the Carters came out of the house carrying the tape player and a lacy pink dress.

"That's the dress that was on the bed!" Violet said. "And the tape player."

The children watched the Carters go back into their own house. "We have to tell

Grandfather and Aunt Jane about this," Henry said. "Come on, let's call home."

The Aldens went back into the house and phoned their grandfather. Jessie quickly told him what had happened and he said, "Just stay in the house. Aunt Jane and I will drive right over. Don't talk to anyone. Just stay there."

"What are we going to do until Grandfather gets here?" Benny asked.

"I know," Violet said. "Let's take some pictures with the camera you brought, Henry."

They tried to forget about the Carters while they took pictures of each other in funny poses. Finally, they heard a car pull up to the house. They ran out to Grandfather and Aunt Jane.

Grandfather looked very serious. "I think we have to talk to the Carters about what you saw and get an explanation from them."

They walked up to the Carters' front door and rang the bell. Mr. Carter answered, looking, as usual, very unfriendly. "Yes?" he said.

"We'd like to come in and talk to you and your wife about something very important," Grandfather said.

"We don't want any visitors," Mr. Carter said.

Then Mrs. Carter appeared behind her husband at the door. "What's going on?" she asked.

"We'd just like a few minutes with you and your husband," Grandfather said.

Mrs. Carter looked at Mr. Alden's serious, unsmiling face and her own face turned pale. She glanced at her husband and then said to the Aldens, "Come in."

They all went into the Carters' living room. "Won't you sit down?" she said to Mr. Alden and Aunt Jane.

They sat and the children stood near them. "Why don't you tell the Carters what has been happening and what you saw," Grandfather said to Jessie.

Jessie began. "All sorts of strange things

have been happening in the Roth house. We found roses we didn't put there. An old dress was on the bed one day — and then it disappeared. A threatening note was in the mailbox. And there was this voice . . . the voice of a girl singing a song. Last night we found a tape player with a tape of the girl's voice. And this morning, Mrs. Carter, we found your sweater on the back stairway. And then . . ." Jessie hesitated, "we saw you and your husband unlocking the back door and going into the house. You came out carrying the tape player and the dress."

Mrs. Carter gasped.

Grandfather said, "Since you knew where the tape player and the dress were, you must have put them there. You have been deliberately trying to frighten my grandchildren. Why? I don't like people upsetting my family."

Mrs. Carter began to weep softly. "I'm so sorry," she said. "I knew this wasn't right."

"I think you'd better explain," Mr. Alden said.

Mr. Carter, now as pale as his wife, began to talk. "It was the house. We had wanted to buy the Roth house and the land for a long time. But we never had enough money to do so. We thought if we made sure the house stayed empty long enough, we would manage to save the money to buy it."

Mrs. Carter took up the story. "When we heard that Joe and Alice Alden had bought the house, we thought that if they could be made to believe the house was haunted, they wouldn't move in. Then we would have a chance to buy the house someday. So we did all the things Jessie mentioned. But I guess the children were smarter than we were."

"What you did wasn't very nice," Benny said. "I really was scared."

"I'm sorry, Benny. I know what we did was wrong," Mrs. Carter said.

"Where did you get a key to the house from?" Violet asked.

"Once the real estate agent gave us a key to let some people in to see the house, on a day she couldn't show it herself. We just made a duplicate of the key."

"The dress, and the roses . . . you did all that?" Violet asked.

"Yes," Mrs. Carter said. "I found that dress in an antique clothing store, and it seemed like the kind of thing Celia might have worn. Mr. Farley had told us about the Roth's beautiful rose garden, so the roses seemed to make sense, too."

"And the singing?" Benny asked directly.

"We used the back stairs to turn on the tape recorder," Mr. Carter explained.

"But *other* people thought the house was haunted," Henry said.

"We started the rumor about the house and Celia's singing years ago," Mr. Carter said. "It worked with some people, like Mr. Farley. And even some people who bought the house didn't stay very long. They just thought that every funny sound that you normally hear in an old house came from a ghost. We were successful for a long time. Until you children came to the house," Mr. Carter said.

"We are sorry. Really. And we do hope your cousins will be very happy here. We really do," Mrs. Carter said.

"I agree with my wife," Mr. Carter said. "I want them to be happy, too. We know what we did was wrong, and I hope we can make it up to you all. If your cousins ever need anything, I hope they'll call on us."

"We accept your apologies," Violet said generously. "There was no real harm done."

The Aldens got into Grandfather's station wagon and they rode home. Jessie was frowning. "What about Celia? Where do you suppose she went? And do you think she is still alive?"

"She would be a very old lady," Aunt Jane said.

"We can't just forget about her," said Violet.

CHAPTER 10

Where is Celia?

After dinner that night, the family gathered in the den. Henry said, "How can we go about trying to find out more about Celia? Even Mr. Farley doesn't know — and he was her neighbor."

"Well, in her letter to her father she said she was going to Bromley to stay with George's parents. Maybe she's still there," Jessie said.

"But she got married. Her name wouldn't be Roth," Henry added.

Aunt Jane was thoughtful. "It doesn't seem likely that she would still be in Bromley after all these years."

"Wait a minute!" Jessie said. She ran over to the bookcase and took Celia's diary from a shelf. She ruffled through it until she came to the page was looking for. "Celia says here: *I told Father last night that I was in love with George Collins.* So Collins would have been her last name if she married George."

"You could try asking information if there's someone by the name of Celia or George Collins living in Bromley," Grandfather suggested. "People in this part of the state often stay in the same town for a lifetime."

Jessie went to the telephone and got information for Bromley. She asked, "Is there a listing for George Collins?"

The operator answered, "I'm sorry we have no one by that name."

"What about the name Celia Collins?" Jessie asked.

There was silence and then the operator returned. "Yes, I have a listing for a Celia Collins. The number is 555-3111."

"I can't believe it," Jessie said. "There *is* a Celia Collins in Bromley."

"Well, why don't you call her?" Benny asked.

Grandfather looked thoughtful. "We must all remember that Mrs. Collins is an old lady. You can't just tell her about her letter on the phone. If you want to call her, Jessie, you have to be careful how you tell the story of what has happened."

"I know, Grandfather," Jessie said. "But I *have* to call her."

Jessie went to the phone and dialed the number she had been given. She waited with her heart beating rapidly as the number rang. Then a voice answered and Jessie said, "I'd like to speak to Mrs. George Collins, please."

A sweet, strong voice said clearly, "This is she."

Jessie quickly told Celia about how they

had become connected with the old Roth house. "Well," Celia Collins said, "I lived there a long time ago."

"We know," Jessie said. "Mrs. Collins, could we come to see you? We have some things we found in the house that I think you would want. I'm sure that my grandfather would drive me and my sister and brothers over to see you. I know that Bromley is not too far from Greenfield. We wouldn't stay too long."

"What kind of things did you find?" Celia asked. Her voice sounded sad.

"I think we should bring them to you," Jessie said.

Mrs. Collins hesitated. Then she said, "All right. Can you come at eleven tomorrow morning?"

The next morning at eleven on the dot the Aldens were seated in Celia Collins's living room. Mrs. Collins was a beautiful woman with short white hair. Her eyes sparkled and her voice was firm.

"Now, you must tell me why you came here," she said.

Violet held out the diary. "We found this in an old box of books."

Mrs. Collins gasped. "My goodness! That diary goes back a long time. It was filled with all the thoughts of a seventeen-year-old. Some not very happy, I recall."

Henry cleared his throat and said, "We found something else. We found this letter jammed in the back of a drawer in a big old desk. The envelope had never been opened because it had gotten stuck in the back of the desk drawer."

Celia Collins's eyes opened wide. "My father never found the letter. Is that what you mean?"

"That's right," Jessie said. "We opened the letter. I hope you don't mind. So, you see, your father never knew where you went."

Tears came to the old lady's eyes. "I never heard from him, so I just thought he didn't want to talk to me. That he was so angry that he was disowning me. It never occurred to me that he hadn't read the letter. I waited and waited to hear from him. Then, after a number of months, I called him. But he had sold the house, and no one knew where he had gone. He was just lost to me."

"You married your George, didn't you?" Violet asked softly.

Celia Collins laughed. "Oh, yes. We married before he went overseas. When he came back, we settled here in Bromley and had three children. He died about ten years ago. My daughter lives just down the block, and I have a housekeeper who lives in this house with me. I was always sad about father, but George and I had a good life together."

Benny said, "Now you know your father wasn't mad at you. He just didn't know where you were."

"That makes me feel much better," Mrs. Collins said. She smiled at the children. "You have made me very happy, and I am delighted to have my diary back."

Grandfather stood up. "We have taken enough of your time. We should leave now."

Mrs. Collins took Violet's hand. "Will all you children come and visit and tell me more about the house?"

"If you'd like," Jessie said. "Someday maybe Grandfather will bring you to your old home so you can see it again."

"That would be my pleasure," Grandfather said.

Mrs. Collins stood and walked to the door with the Aldens. "Someday I will call you, and my housekeeper can drive me to the old house. I would like to see it again and to meet your cousins."

She kissed each of the children and shook Grandfather's hand. "I can't thank you enough for giving me back my father."

The Aldens got into Grandfather's car and rode in silence for a while. Then Jessie said, "I'm so glad we found Celia."

One month later, on a warm Sunday afternoon, there was a party going on at the old Roth house. Joe and Alice were having a housewarming party. There were platters of food and cookies and cakes on the dining room table. The living room was filled with flowers, and the house was filled with people.

All the Aldens were there and Aunt Jane and Uncle Andy. Joe and Alice had also invited Mr. Farley, Ms. Evans, Thomas Yeats, and even the Carters. The Carters, who felt so sorry that they had tried to keep Joe and Alice from moving in, had become perfect neighbors. They were helpful and welcoming. But the person whom everyone was waiting for was Celia Roth Collins. She had been invited and had said that her housekeeper would drive her over.

The moment came, and Celia Collins walked into the house she had not been in for decades. Alice ran to the door to welcome her and led her into the living room. As Mrs. Collins looked around, tears came to her eyes. "The house looks beautiful," she said to Alice.

Alice said, "Let me introduce you to everyone. You know the Aldens. And this is the children's aunt and uncle." Then she reached Mr. Farley. He looked at Celia and asked, "Do you remember me at all?"

Celia Collins stared at him. "Well, it's been a long, long time but you do look a little like a boy who lived next door to me. He was a real imp. His name was Charlie Farley."

Mr. Farley smiled broadly. "That was me! You know, Mrs. Collins, I had a real crush on you when I was a boy."

Mrs. Collins smiled, too. "I knew that, Charlie."

Mr. Farley looked thoughtful. "I think that was why I wanted to believe your ghost was still in the house. Just so I could pretend you were still here."

Alice took Celia over to Mr. Yeats. "Mr. Yeats is painting a picture of the house," she said.

"Yes, I wanted the house not to change so I could finish the painting. When the children started fixing the place up, I was so angry. I was afraid all my work would be wasted. I even asked Mr. Farley to keep an eye on the children for me — let me know what they were up to. He refused, and rightly so. Anyway, I did finish the painting."

"Perhaps," Mrs. Collins said, "you would sell it to me."

Mr. Yeats bowed slightly. "Madam, it would be a pleasure if you would let me give the painting to you as a gift."

"I would love that," Mrs. Collins replied.

The last one Alice introduced Celia to was Terry Evans. "Ms. Evans is writing a history of Greenfield."

"Yes," Ms. Evans said, "and this house will have a chapter all to itself. I wanted it to become a landmark but Joe and Alice have fixed it up so beautifully. It is as well cared for as if it were a landmark."

Everybody sat down and Celia Collins sighed. "Everything would be perfect if I just knew what happened to my father."

Ms. Evans jumped up. "I know that. I have been doing research on the families that lived in this house."

Mrs. Collins looked startled. "What happened to him?"

Ms. Evans walked over to Celia and sat down on the sofa next to her. "What I discovered is that he moved to Boston a few months after you disappeared. He tried in many ways to find you. He finally put an ad in a Boston paper, hoping you might see it. I wrote it out and brought a copy of it for you."

Celia's hand trembled as she reached for it. Then she dropped her hand and said to Ms. Evans, "I think you had better read it to me."

Ms. Evans cleared her throat and read: "*For Celia Roth, my daughter: I know that you must have married George Collins and that is why you left home. I was wrong to try to stop you from marrying George. He is a nice young man and you deserve to be happy with him. Please write to me at the box number below if you see this ad. If I*

*don't hear from you I will know you never read
this paper. I know that you love me, as I love you,
and would reply if you could. Your loving father,
Robert Roth.*"

There was a silence in the room after Ms.
Evans stopped reading. Then Mr. Alden
said, "So now you know, Mrs. Collins, that
your father forgave you and knew that you
loved him."

"I am so glad," Mrs. Collins said, wiping
the tears from her eyes. "I will always be
grateful to all of you," she said, looking
around the room.

"Can we eat now?" Benny asked.

Everyone laughed and Alice said, "There's
a lot of food in the dining room. Benny is
right. It's time to eat."

Everyone walked into the dining room and
filled their plates. Mrs. Collins's housekeeper
fixed a plate for the old woman, who remained seated in the living room. The housekeeper looked at the Alden children and said,
"I don't think you can know how happy you
have made Mrs. Collins. Now she can stop

worrying about what happened between her and her father."

Back in the living room, they all ate the wonderful food Alice and Joe had prepared. Benny sat on the floor next to Mrs. Collins and said, "Would you come and visit *us* sometime? I'd like to show you our boxcar. You know *we* ran away once, too."

Mrs. Collins smiled. "Benny, I would love to visit you and to hear about your adventures."

"We've had lots of them," Violet said. "But you know, I think this one was the best."

GERTRUDE CHANDLER WARNER discovered when she was teaching that many readers who like an exciting story could find no books that were both easy and fun to read. She decided to try to meet this need, and her first book, *The Boxcar Children*, quickly proved she had succeeded.

Miss Warner drew on her own experiences to write each mystery. As a child she spent hours watching trains go by on the tracks opposite her family home. She often dreamed about what it would be like to set up housekeeping in a caboose or freight car — the situation the Alden children find themselves in.

When Miss Warner received requests for more adventures involving Henry, Jessie, Violet, and Benny Alden, she began additional stories. In each, she chose a special setting and introduced unusual or eccentric characters who liked the unpredictable.

While the mystery element is central to each of Miss Warner's books, she never thought of them as strictly juvenile mysteries. She liked to stress the Aldens' independence and resourcefulness and their solid New England devotion to using up and making do. The Aldens go about most of their adventures with as little adult supervision as possible — something else that delights young readers.

Miss Warner lived in Putnam, Connecticut, until her death in 1979. During her lifetime, she received hundreds of letters from girls and boys telling her how much they liked her books.